Electro's Gotta Glow

Adapted by Steve Behling
Based on the episode written by Mike Kubat
Illustrated by Premise Entertainment

Los Angeles • New York

SUSTAINABLE FORESTRY INITIATIVE
Certified Sourcing
www.sfiprogram.org
SFI-01415

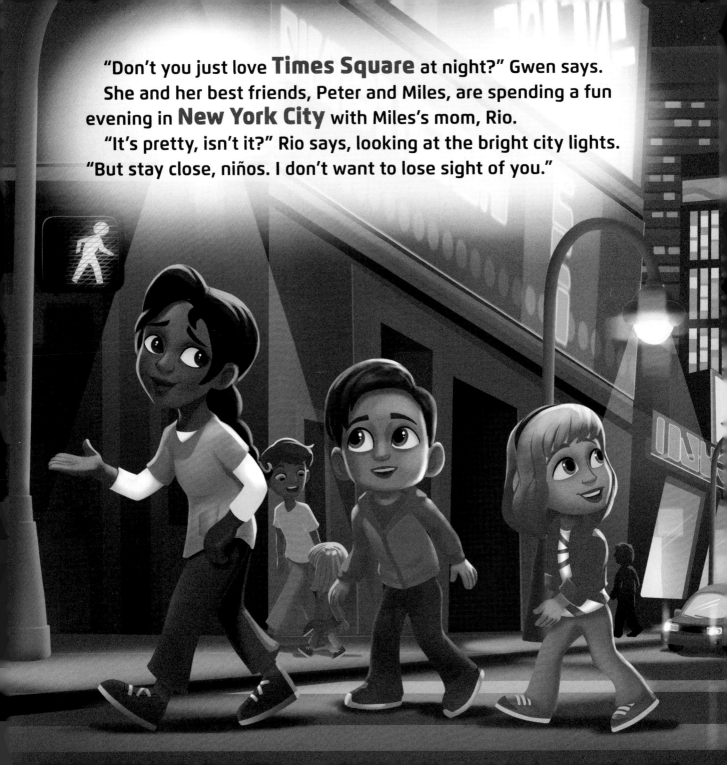

"Don't you just love **Times Square** at night?" Gwen says. She and her best friends, Peter and Miles, are spending a fun evening in **New York City** with Miles's mom, Rio.

"It's pretty, isn't it?" Rio says, looking at the bright city lights. "But stay close, niños. I don't want to lose sight of you."

Speaking of losing sight, where is Miles? Uh-oh—he is paying more attention to his video game than he is to walking!

Rio takes Peter, Gwen, and Miles to **Yo-Ho Yogurt**. It's an awesome pirate-themed shop that sells delicious frozen yogurt!

"**Pirates** and **yogurt**?" Peter says.
"Count me in!" Miles says.
They get a table while Rio goes inside the shop to order.

But someone else has come to Times Square, and she doesn't want frozen yogurt. It's **Electro**!

"I'm going to steal all the electricity in this city with my trusty Electro-Zorber," Electro says.

Electro can't wait to steal all the electricity, so she zips into the middle of Times Square.

"Look out!" someone shouts.

"It's Electro!" someone else yells. "Run!"

"All righty," Electro says. "This looks like a good place!"

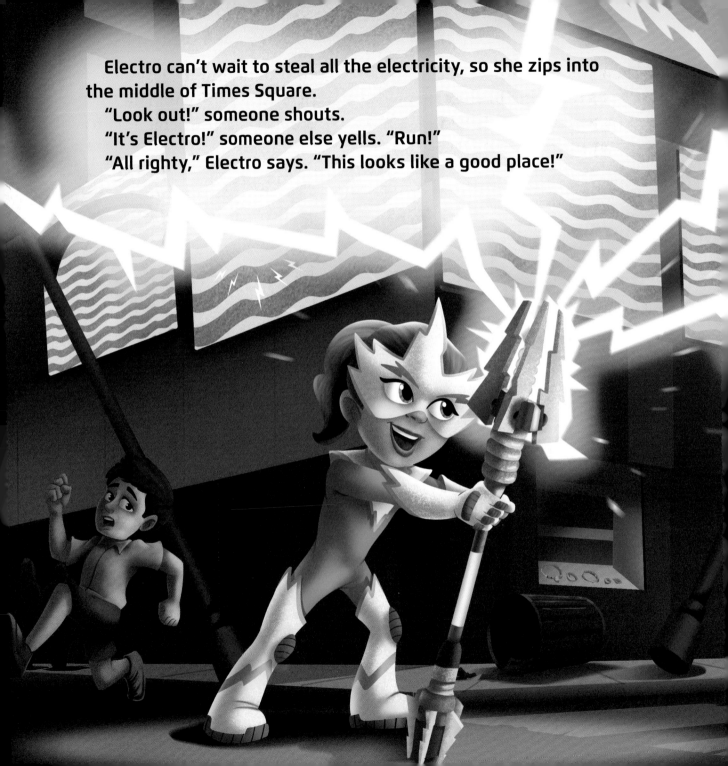

Then she jabs her **Electro-Zorber** into the ground. The device glows as it begins to soak up all the electricity from the city. The energy will be stored inside the Electro-Zorber. Electro will be able to use that power whenever she wants!

Electro laughs as lights all over the city start to go out.
Peter, Gwen, and Miles watch from outside the frozen yogurt shop.
Suddenly, Gwen says, "Whoa, look at that!"
The kids see Electro rising above Times Square. She tells everyone that she stole **all the electricity**.
"We've got to stop her!" Peter says.

Changing into their Super Hero costumes, Spidey, Ghost-Spider, and Miles get ready to swing into action.

But just as Spidey thwips a web, he hears someone crying.

"Help, I dropped my Wubby!" a little girl says, walking with her mom. "I can't find my Wubby!"

"That little girl lost her toy," Spidey says. "You two go on while I help her."

Ghost-Spider and Miles get ready to stop Electro, but there are more cries for help!

"I fell in a manhole!" someone yells. With **no lights** anywhere, the person couldn't see and fell in the hole!

Ghost-Spider helps the person climb out.

Meanwhile, Miles hears his mom calling his name! She is worried about him, Peter, and Gwen, because she can't see them.

Swinging down on his web, Miles tells his mom that Team Spidey took the kids to safety.

Using the light on his comm link,
Spidey helps find the little girl's lost toy.
"My Wubby!" she says. She grabs
the toy and hugs it tightly.
"Thanks, Spidey!" her mom says.

The three Super Heroes meet up. While they were helping people stuck in the dark, Electro escaped with her power-packed Electro-Zorber!

"We've got to get the lights back on," Miles says.

"How can we do that when Electro has all the **electricity**?" Gwen asks.

But then Peter remembers that Electro doesn't have *all* the electricity. Their Spidey gadgets and vehicles run on their own power!

So Spidey uses his comm link to call their computer, WEB-STER.

Back at WEB-Quarters, a secret door opens.
"Launching **Team Transport**," says WEB-STER.
The Team Transport flies up into the night sky, ready to help our heroes!

Soon the Team Transport arrives in Times Square.

Spidey has an idea: they can use electricity from the Team Transport to **charge up** their suits. They can even charge their webs! Maybe then they can spread some light around the city so people will be able to see.

Three charging cables descend from the Team Transport.

"Are you ready?" Spidey asks.

Each hero attaches a charging cable to their costume. **"Let's power up!"** Ghost-Spider says.

"Whoa!" Miles exclaims as his costume starts to glow. **"Light-up suits!"** Ghost-Spider says.

Then Spidey thwips a web that **glows** just like their suits.
"Glow webs?" Miles says, impressed. "Sweet!"
"Let's brighten things up around here," Ghost-Spider says.

THWIP! THWIP! THWIP!
Team Spidey thwips webs across Times Square. The webs
weave everywhere, glowing brightly, so everyone can see
where they are going.
"Glow-webs-glow!" Team Spidey shouts.

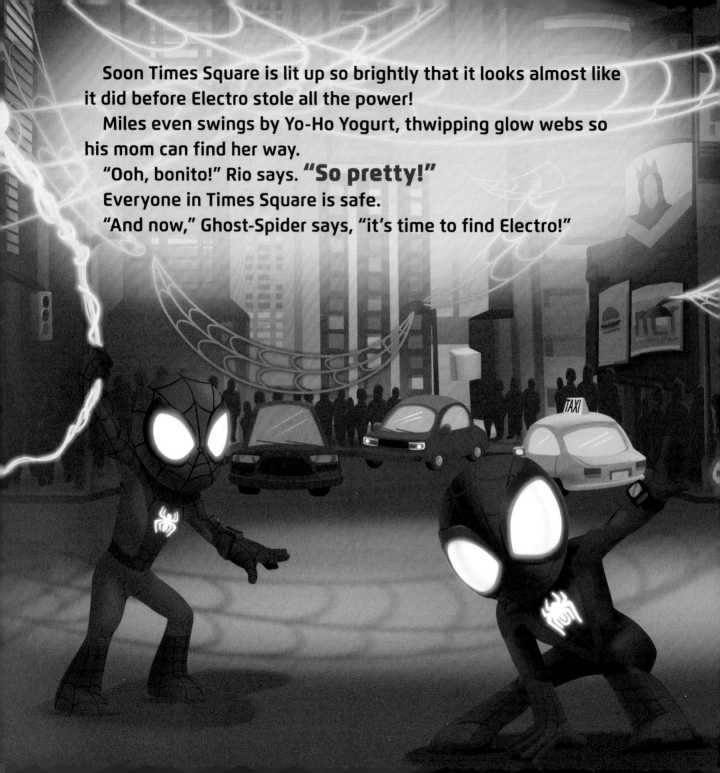

Soon Times Square is lit up so brightly that it looks almost like it did before Electro stole all the power!

Miles even swings by Yo-Ho Yogurt, thwipping glow webs so his mom can find her way.

"Ooh, bonito!" Rio says. **"So pretty!"**

Everyone in Times Square is safe.

"And now," Ghost-Spider says, "it's time to find Electro!"

But where could Electro be hiding?
"Electro and her Electro-Zorber are full of electricity," Ghost-Spider says. "All that electricity will be glowing brightly. . . . "

The heroes' search leads them to a brightly lit warehouse. Inside, Electro is **charging up** with her Electro-Zorber!

"Hiya, Electro!" Spidey says as he drops inside the warehouse.

Electro stares at Spidey's glowing suit. She wants that electricity, too!

"Gotta catch me first!" Spidey says as Electro hurls an energy sphere at him.

But Spidey is too quick, and Electro misses!

"Yoo-hoo!" Ghost-Spider says.

Electro wants to steal her suit's electricity, too!

Electro is so busy trying to catch Spidey and Ghost-Spider that she forgets all about her **Electro-Zorber**!

Unnoticed, Miles thwips his webs and takes the Electro-Zorber.

Just as Electro is about to zap Spidey and Ghost-Spider, her power begins to fade.

She goes to recharge at the Electro-Zorber, but it's gone!

Electro sees Miles carrying off her device.

She tries to stop him, but her electricity goes out altogether, and she falls.

Ghost-Spider and Spidey thwip their webs and catch Electro.

"You defeated me!" Electro says.

With Electro captured, Team Spidey returns to Times Square with the Electro-Zorber.

They place the Electro-Zorber in the ground. All at once, electricity returns to the streetlights and buildings.

"That's more like it!" Ghost-Spider says.

"Now let's get back to my mom!" Miles says.

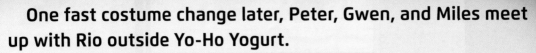

One fast costume change later, Peter, Gwen, and Miles meet up with Rio outside Yo-Ho Yogurt.

"Oh, thank goodness you're all safe," Rio says. "Team Spidey promised you would be."

"Just a little hungry, maybe," Miles says. "How about some frozen yogurt?"

"Oh, I'm sorry, niños. Unfortunately, it all melted!" Rio says.

But the kids don't care—they think that **yogurt shakes** taste just as yummy!